PEOPLE of CORN
A Mayan Story

Retold by
MARY-JOAN GERSON

Pictures by
CARLA GOLEMBE

Little, Brown and Company

Boston   New York   Toronto   London

To my children, Daniel and Jessica, for dreaming, playing, and believing.
M.G.

To David, Marilyn, and Noah Stern with love.
I painted many of these pictures during my Artist-in-Residency at the Fundación Centro Cultural, Altos de Chaven, Republica Dominicana. Muchas grácias to the Fundación for my Residency, which allowed me to create in a magical place, and to so many people there, especially Stephen Kaplan.
C.G.

Text copyright © 1995 by Mary-Joan Gerson
Illustrations copyright © 1995 by Carla Golembe

First Edition
The excerpt on the last page of this book is from *The Popol Vuh: The Mayan Book of the Dawn of Life,* translated by Dennis Tetlock. New York: Touchstone/Simon and Schuster, 1985. Reprinted by permission of the Balkan Agency.

Library of Congress Cataloging-in-Publication Data
People of corn : a Mayan story / retold by Mary-Joan Gerson ; pictures by Carla Golembe. — 1st ed.
    p.   cm.
Summary: After several unsuccessful attempts to create grateful creatures, the Mayan gods use sacred corn to fashion a people who will thank and praise their creators.
ISBN 0-316-30854-4
1. Mayas — Folklore. 2. Maya mythology. 3. Corn — Folklore.
[1. Mayas — Folklore. 2. Indians of Central America — Folklore.
3. Folklore — Guatemala. 4. Creation — Folklore. 5. Corn — Folklore.]
I. Gerson, Mary-Joan. II. Golembe, Carla, ill.
F1435.3.F6P46 1995
[398.2'089974] — dc20   94-18140

10 9 8 7 6 5 4 3 2 1

NIL

Published simultaneously in Canada
by Little, Brown & Company (Canada) Limited
and in Great Britain by Little, Brown and Company (UK) Limited

Printed in Italy

The pictures in this book were painted in gouache, an opaque water-based paint, on Victoria cover, a 100-percent rag black paper.

Author's Note

This tale is from the Maya, a people whose culture began in Mexico and Central America more than three thousand years ago. Sometime between 2000 and 1000 B.C., the Maya discovered corn — and with it, the art of farming. This discovery meant that they no longer had to wander in search of food but instead could plant corn, which became their principal food, in the same fields year after year. They were now able to begin the creation of their remarkable civilization.

They built cities in the jungle with open stone plazas surrounded by enormous pyramids. They fashioned palaces, painted them in brilliant colors, and carved figures in feathered headdresses into the walls. At the height of their kingdom, they controlled an area six times the size of ancient Rome. And they learned to map the stars and planets long before the Europeans could.

No one knows exactly why the ancient Maya suddenly disappeared around A.D. 800. However, this tale of creation survived and is still told in villages today. In this tale, unlike most creation stories, the gods first try and fail, then try and fail again, before they finally succeed. You can find in this story some of the most important Mayan beliefs. The first is that the roots of all living things are connected. For the Maya say that if you cut down a tree, you must ask forgiveness or a star will fall out of the sky. Another belief shown in the story is that, for the Maya, sleeping and dreaming provide a pathway into the world of the gods from whence we came.

To the Maya, everything in the world is part of one life force. The fate of everything — dreams and real life, animals and people, mountains and stars — is bound together in the endless flow of time.

Let me tell you about the Mayan people living in the highlands of Guatemala. Let me tell you about their corn, which grows dry and straight and strong. To the Maya, each full crop of corn is like a miracle. In the early spring, the villagers burn incense to purify the fields before the corn is planted, to make sure that it will grow. Later, during summer storms, they call out to their plants to comfort them. You see, the Maya believe that corn, like all plants, has an inner life and soul.

In the fall, when the golden corn is finally harvested, the people carry it back to their villages in sacred processions, firing colored lights to the heavens in gratitude.

From this harvest, the Mayan people make tortillas, tamales, and tacos, which they fill with spicy meat sauce or black beans. They make *atolé,* a hot drink of ground corn sweetened with honey. These most important foods keep them strong enough to work on the steep highland hills, and strong enough to walk miles and miles, carrying huge baskets of food and firewood on their heads and backs.

But corn is much more than food for the Maya — it is the spirit of life itself. You see, the Maya believe that long ago when the world began, the first people on earth were actually made from corn. This is how it happened:

In the beginning, the Maya say, there was a deep, dark silence that seemed more like an ending than a beginning. In the empty sky there were no birds. In the black, swaying seas there were no fish. There were no mountains and no caverns, and most of all, there were no people.

Against the blackness of nothing, the light of the gods was dazzling and clear. One day the two gods of all creation — Plumed Serpent and Heart of Sky — decided to create life.

The gods talked and planned together for a long time. They drew maps and pictures that spread across the sky. Finally they were ready.

The formation of the earth was strange, magical, and wonderful. At first there was only fog and clouds. Then the mountains sprouted in the seas, and the trees spread across them, forming woods and forests. At last the gods created living creatures to dwell in the forests and in the seas: pumas and monkeys, dolphins, sea turtles, and fish. "You wild beasts of the fields shall drink from the rivers, sleep in the canyons, and rest on the meadows," said the gods, "and you birds shall fly through the branches of the trees."

When they finished, Plumed Serpent and Heart of Sky realized they had the same wish. They wanted to be thanked for their work. So, stretching across the sky one morning, they appeared to all the creatures and said, "Now you must speak and understand one another. And then say our names, so that we may be honored in heaven, since we are your father and your mother."

But the birds and the fish and the animals, try as they may, could not speak. They could only cackle and chirp and bellow.

When the gods saw that their creatures could not pronounce their names and could not talk about them in story and song, they were unhappy. Who would remember the beginning of the earth? Who would celebrate the gift of life?

Plumed Serpent and Heart of Sky decided to begin again. This time, on the new day of creation, they traveled beyond the heavens to visit the grandmother of the sun, who was called Grandmother of Light.

The great goddess was sitting at her giant loom weaving a cloth so beautiful that Plumed Serpent and Heart of Sky were speechless at the sight of it. It was the cloth of life, being woven right in front of their eyes. They stood silently, watching Grandmother of Light, and her dancing hands gave them hope. "We, too, will use our own hands to create life, and we will make something strong — puppet creatures made of wood! And this time we will make sure our creatures can speak."

Soon the earth was filled with talking wooden people. Because they could all speak, the rulers could give orders, and the workers understood and obeyed. They built wide bridges and long roads and deep canals, and the land began to prosper.

But nowhere amidst the hum of labor and cheers of success were there songs of praise. Not once did the puppet people thank their creators for giving them life.

"Now how have we failed?" cried Plumed Serpent and Heart of Sky. And then they realized their mistake. The wooden puppet people could work without rest because they had no blood in their veins, no breath in their lungs. But they also had no hearts, and without hearts, they could never love their creators. They could never truly celebrate what they made or what was made for them by the gods.

"Will our work of creation never be finished?" thundered the gods as they burst the rain clouds and heaved the seas so that a great flood cleansed the earth of the people without hearts.

For a long time, there was a thick blackness in the sky and rain fell day and night. The land was flooded, and the crops rotted. The animals and birds scattered to the distant hills and valleys to search for food and dry shelter.

And then one morning, four creatures at the edge of starvation — Fox, Coyote, Parrot, and Crow — discovered something magical at the very same moment. Climbing over the highest mountain at the farthest reaches of the earth, they found a field in which hundreds of white-and-yellow ears of corn grew dry and straight and strong. And as their eyes feasted on the sight, a thread of life was spun from their eyes to the souls of Plumed Serpent and Heart of Sky.

At once the gods knew that this was the true source of life, planted in mystery by Grandmother of Light. The two gods gathered the sacred corn, then ground it and mixed it with water and fashioned the first true people, the mother-fathers of the Maya.

And indeed these people of corn were filled with the wonder of the earth. Like the animals, they could run across the fields and climb the mountains. Like the wooden people, they could speak to one another and build bridges and roads. But unlike the animals and wooden puppets, the people of corn could thank and praise their creators because they had both hearts and voices. With their hearts they built immense pyramids of carved and colored stone to honor their creators. And with their voices they told the story of creation over and over, so all the children would remember it and tell it to their children. They danced and beat their drums of celebration at dawn and noon and sunset.

But the gods grew worried. Would the people of corn forget their birth in the hands of Plumed Serpent and Heart of Sky? Perhaps, thought the gods, these people knew and saw too much.

So they questioned the people of corn. "What do you think of the senses you have received? How far can you see across the land?" They answered, "Indeed we can see both what is near and what is far, even into the mountains and through the ocean depths. We visit the gods of heaven and the lords of the underworld."

Plumed Serpent and Heart of Sky were stunned. These people had the wisdom of the gods! Heart of Sky flashed a jolt of lightning across the sky, but the people of corn felt no fear. Plumed Serpent covered the sun with his wings, but the people below barely trembled in the frozen air.

It was then that the gods realized they still had not finished their work of creation. In no time these godlike people would tire of being thankful for their lives and for the corn that gave birth to them. And so in one last act of creation, the gods veiled the eyes of the corn people, so that they could no longer see beyond their own time and place. In that one moment the eyes of every living person became clouded, like a valley covered in early morning mist. From then on, the corn people could see only what was near and real.

But as the roots of all living things are one, the gods could not take every bit of magic away from their people. And so the Mayan children and their parents believe that at night when they go to sleep, the gods lift the veil over their eyes and in their dreams they see deep into the center of the world. They travel to the far world of heaven and visit the gods and see the fields of bright and sacred corn that gave birth to them. And what they see they remember with their hearts and their hands. For even today, Mayan women will tell you that the designs they weave into their cloth come from the gods, from the beginning of the world, and that these patterns first appear to them when they are fast asleep, wandering in a world of dreams.

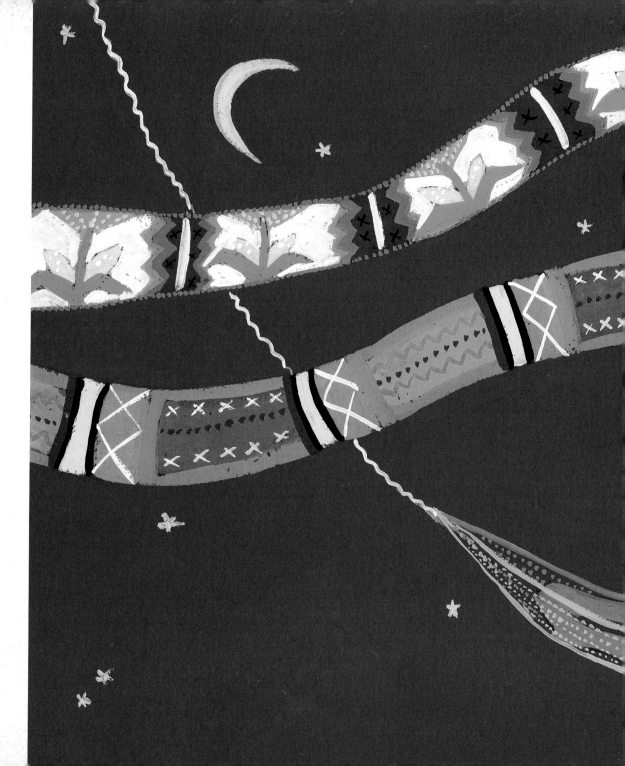

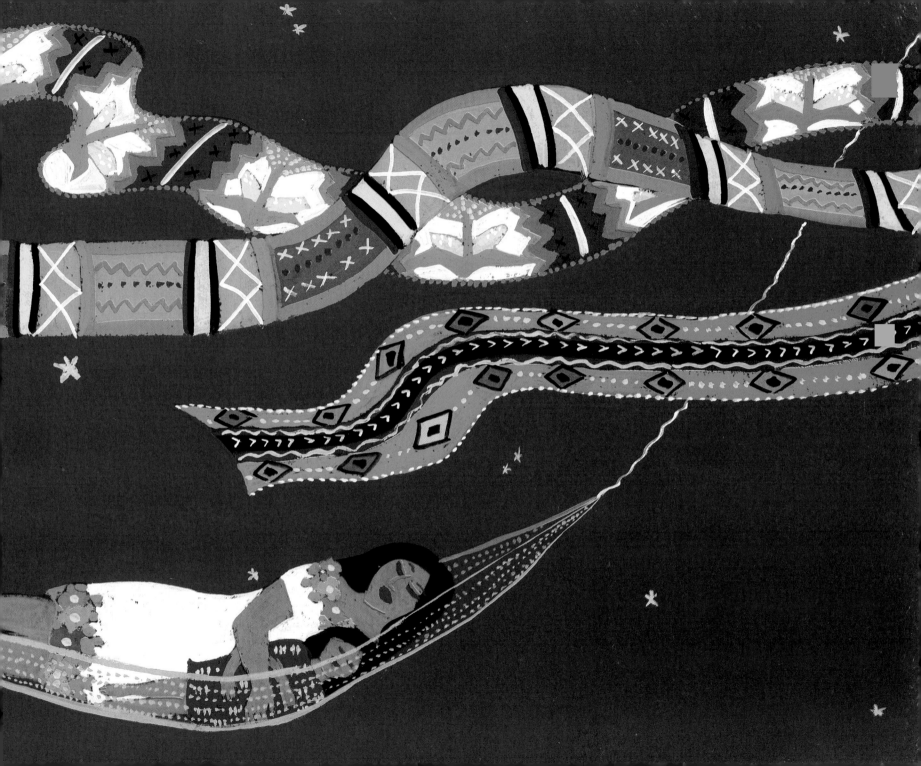

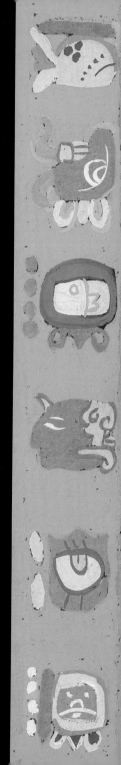

Source Note

The Spanish explorers who conquered the Maya in 1524 forbade them from telling their ancient stories and practicing their religion. A brave group of them, however, from Quiche, Guatemala, learned European script and wrote down their myths. They collected their writings in a sacred book called the *Popol Vuh*, which means "council book," and that is where this tale was first recorded. In the present telling, events have been connected in a more modern flowing narrative, but the depictions and sequences of the ancient text have, in all cases, been retained.

by the Maker, Modeler,
mother-father of life, of humankind,
giver of breath, giver of heart,
bearer, upbringer in the light that lasts
of those born in the light, begotten in the light;
worrier, knower of everything, whatever there is:
sky-earth, lake-sea

From the *Popol Vuh*